THE BOOK
THAT
JACK WROTE

Written by Jon Scieszka
Paintings by Daniel Adel

VIKING

This is the Book that Jack wrote.

THE BO
THAT
JACK WROTE

Written by Jon Scieszka
Paintings by Daniel Adel

This is the Picture

That lay in the Book that Jack wrote.

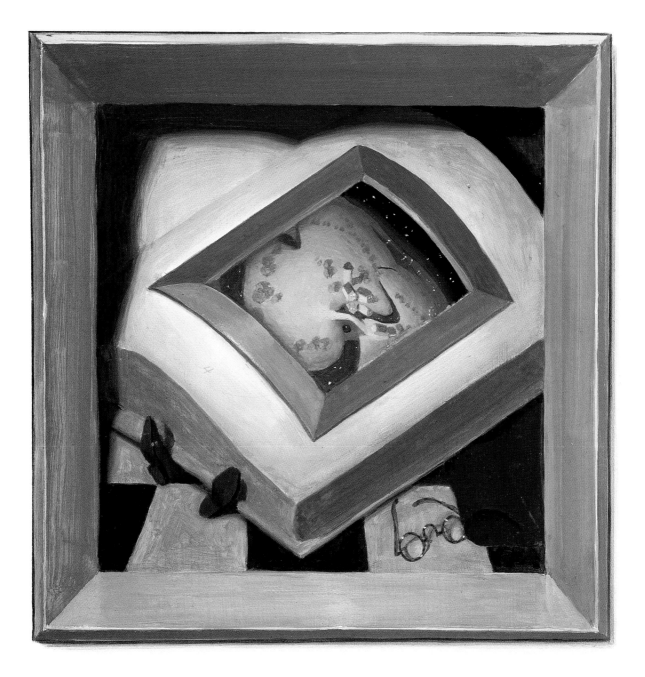

This is the Rat,

That fell in the Picture

That lay in the Book that Jack wrote.

This is the Cat,

That ate the Rat,

That fell in the Picture

That lay in the Book that Jack wrote.

This is the Dog,

That chased the Cat,

That ate the Rat,

That fell in the Picture

That lay in the Book that Jack wrote.

This is the Cow sailing over the moon,

That spooked the Dog,

That chased the Cat,

That ate the Rat,

That fell in the Picture

That lay in the Book that Jack wrote.

This is the Baby humming the tune,

That tossed the Cow sailing over the moon,

That spooked the Dog,

That chased the Cat,

That ate the Rat,

That fell in the Picture

That lay in the Book that Jack wrote.

This is the Pie flying through the air,

That beaned the Baby humming the tune,

That tossed the Cow sailing over the moon,

That spooked the Dog,

That chased the Cat,

That ate the Rat,

That fell in the Picture

That lay in the Book that Jack wrote.

This is the Pieman at the fair,

That flung the Pie flying through the air,

That beaned the Baby humming the tune,

That tossed the Cow sailing over the moon,

That spooked the Dog,

That chased the Cat,

That ate the Rat,

That fell in the Picture

That lay in the Book that Jack wrote.

This is the Egg falling off the wall,

That startled the Pieman at the fair,

That flung the Pie flying through the air,

That beaned the Baby humming the tune,

That tossed the Cow sailing over the moon,

That spooked the Dog,

That chased the Cat,

That ate the Rat,

That fell in the Picture

That lay in the Book that Jack wrote.

PIES

This is the Hatter in the hall,

That knocked the Egg falling off the wall,

That startled the Pieman at the fair,

That flung the Pie flying through the air,

That beaned the Baby humming the tune,

That tossed the Cow sailing over the moon,

That spooked the Dog,

That chased the Cat,

That ate the Rat,

That fell in the Picture

That lay in the Book that Jack wrote.

This is the Bug, that frayed the rug,

That tripped the Hatter in the hall,

That knocked the Egg falling off the wall,

That startled the Pieman at the fair,

That flung the Pie flying through the air,

That beaned the Baby humming the tune,

That tossed the Cow sailing over the moon,

That spooked the Dog,

That chased the Cat,

That ate the Rat,

That fell in the Picture

That lay in the Book that Jack wrote.

This is the Man in the tattered coat,

That stomped the Bug, that frayed the rug,

That tripped the Hatter in the hall,

That knocked the Egg falling off the wall,

That startled the Pieman at the fair,

That flung the Pie flying through the air,

That beaned the Baby humming the tune,

That tossed the Cow sailing over the moon,

That spooked the Dog,

That chased the Cat,

That ate the Rat,

That fell in the Picture

That lay in the Book that Jack wrote.

This is the Book that Jack wrote,

That squashed the Man in the tattered coat,

That stomped the Bug, that frayed the rug,

That tripped the Hatter in the hall,

That knocked the Egg falling off the wall,

That startled the Pieman at the fair,

That flung the Pie flying through the air,

That beaned the Baby humming the tune,

That tossed the Cow sailing over the moon,

That spooked the Dog,

That chased the Cat,

That ate the Rat,

That fell in the Picture...

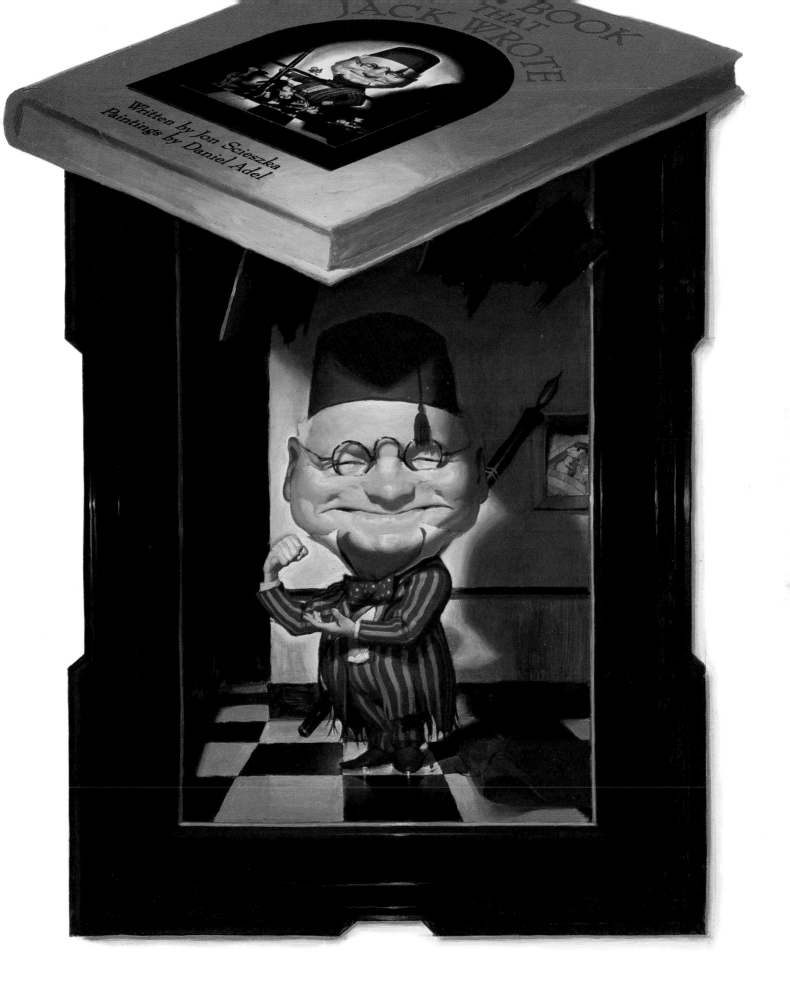

That lay in the Book that Jack wrote.